# Daisy Dawson

## at the Seaside

# Daisy Dawson

## at the Seaside

# Steve Voake

illustrated by Jessica Meserve

WALKER
BOOKS

This is a work of fiction. Names, characters, places and incidents are either the product of the author's imagination or, if real, used fictitiously.

First published 2011 by Walker Books Ltd
87 Vauxhall Walk, London SE11 5HJ

2 4 6 8 10 9 7 5 3 1

Text © 2011 Steve Voake
Illustrations © 2011 Jessica Meserve

The right of Steve Voake and Jessica Meserve to be identified as author and illustrator respectively of this work has been asserted by them in accordance with the Copyright, Designs and Patents Act 1988

This book has been typeset in StempelSchneidler

Printed and bound in Great Britain by Clays Ltd, St Ives plc

British Library Cataloguing in Publication Data:
a catalogue record for this book is available from the British Library

ISBN 978-1-4063-2747-2

www.walker.co.uk

*For Gill Evans*
*S.V.*

*For Elodie*
*J.M.*

# Summer Holidays

It was the last day of term and Daisy was saying goodbye to the school gerbils, Burble and Furball.

"Can't we stay with you for the summer?" asked Furball. "We could get the squirrels round for a sleepover and watch films about gerbils who save the world."

"Can't I'm afraid," said Daisy, "I'm going away on holiday tomorrow, so Abigail's going to look after you."

"Has she got any films about gerbils saving the world?" asked Burble.

"I don't think so," said Daisy, "but she has got popcorn."

"Ooh," said Furball, "I like her already."

"It doesn't take much to make him happy," said Burble. She waved at Daisy through the bars. "Have a great summer, Daisy D!"

"You too!" said Daisy.

As she walked home, she noticed Trixie the cat sneaking through the long grass towards Flapperton the sparrow. Daisy had made friends with Flapperton only that morning when she had given him some of her flapjack.

"Hey, Trixie!" she called as loudly as she could. "What are you up to?"

As Flapperton squawked
and flew up into the
trees, Trixie stared
at Daisy with cool
green eyes.

"Thanks a bunch,
Daisy," she said. "How would
you like it if I came round to your
place and scared your dinner away?"

Daisy smiled sweetly. "You're welcome
to try," she said, "but I don't think jam
sandwiches scare easily."

"You didn't upset her, did you?"
chuckled Boom the dog as Trixie slunk
away into the long grass. "I do so hate it
when cats get upset."

He put his paws on the gate and rested his chin on the warm wood. "How was school?"

"Finished for the summer," said Daisy. "Which means I can go swimming every day instead!"

"Swimming!" echoed a voice from somewhere in the old oak tree.

There was a loud splash and Daisy turned to see a small squirrel climb out of the water trough. As he shook himself and waved, another squirrel belly-flopped into the water behind him.

"Splashdown!" shouted the first squirrel, clapping his paws together. "The squirrel has landed!"

"Hazel and Conker!" cried Daisy as Hazel swam to the side and tumbled out onto the grass.

"Hello Daisy," said Conker, squeezing the water out of his tail. "Fancy a swim?"

"Thanks for the offer," said Daisy, "but I think I'll wait until I get to the seaside."

"Seaside?" said Hazel, drying herself with a dock leaf. "What's a seaside?"

"You know," said Conker. "That thing in the park that goes up and down."

"The sun?" said Hazel.

"I think he means a seesaw," said Daisy.

"That's it," said Conker. "I've always wanted a go on one."

"I'm talking about the sea*side*," explained Daisy patiently. "It's a place with water and boats and ice cream."

"Is it very scary at the seaside?" asked Hazel.

"No, it's lovely," said Daisy. "Why?"

"Because you said it makes you scream."

"Huh?" said Conker.

"You said 'It's a place with lots of boats and water and I scream'."

"No, not 'I scream'," said Daisy. "Ice cream."

"I know. That's what I said."

Daisy shook her head. "No, *ice cream*. You know when the water trough freezes over in winter?"

"Uh-huh."

"Well it's a bit like that."

"Can you skate on it?"

"Not really. You sort of … eat it."

"Wow," said Conker. "This seaside place is *mad*." He stared at Daisy for a moment and then asked, "Where's that funny thing where you put all your stuff?"

Daisy glanced over her shoulder and realized that Conker was talking about her backpack.

"I don't need it," she said. "I'm not going to school today."

"Me neither," said Conker.

"You never go," said Hazel.

"Good point," said Conker.

At that moment, Meadowsweet the mare trotted out from beneath the oak tree and leaned over the fence to nuzzle Daisy's hair.

"Hello Meadowsweet," said Daisy. "I was just telling everyone that I'm off to the seaside tomorrow."

"How lovely," said Meadowsweet. "I knew a donkey who went there once. He wore a straw hat to keep the sun off his head and he used to let the children ride around on his back."

"That sounds like fun," said Conker, looking up at Meadowsweet.

"Don't get any ideas young squirrel," said Meadowsweet. "It's too hot for that kind of thing."

"Is the sea as big as the river?" asked Boom.

"It's bigger than the river," said Daisy. "Sometimes you can see the whole of the sky in it."

*The whole of the sky,"* whispered Hazel. "Imagine that."

Daisy saw that Boom was looking worried and remembered Meadowsweet telling her that he had once fallen into deep water as a puppy.

"Don't worry Boom," she said. "I'm a very good swimmer."

As she knelt down and stroked his ears, he whispered, "The sea's a big place, Daisy. Promise me if you ever get lost in it, you'll swim towards the sun."

"The sun?" Daisy frowned. "Why?"

"Because the sun's above the field," said Boom. "And if you swim towards it, you'll find your way home."

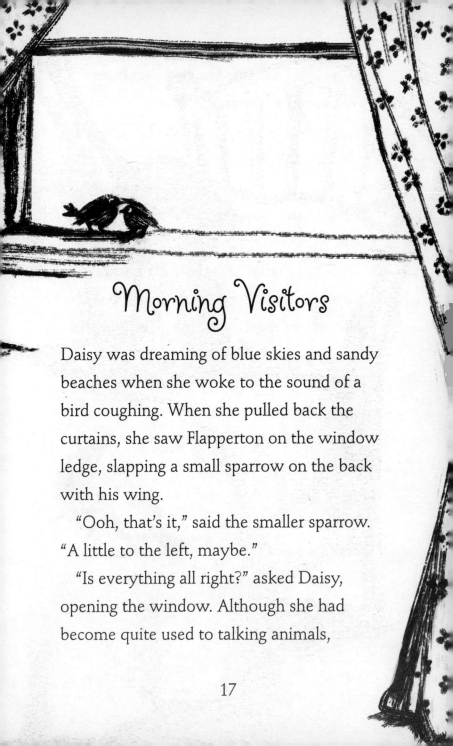

# Morning Visitors

Daisy was dreaming of blue skies and sandy beaches when she woke to the sound of a bird coughing. When she pulled back the curtains, she saw Flapperton on the window ledge, slapping a small sparrow on the back with his wing.

"Ooh, that's it," said the smaller sparrow. "A little to the left, maybe."

"Is everything all right?" asked Daisy, opening the window. Although she had become quite used to talking animals,

this was the first time she had ever been
woken up by a coughing sparrow.

"Oh hi, Daisy," said Flapperton. "Thanks
for saving me from that cat yesterday by the
way."

"That's OK," said Daisy. "What's the
matter with your friend?"

"It's a toast crust," Flapperton explained.
"Harry here tried to eat a whole one but
it got stuck in his throat. Isn't that right,
Harry?"

Harry nodded and coughed a bit more.
Then he put his wing over his beak,
because his mother had taught
him that this was the polite
thing to do.

"Hang on," said Daisy.
"Won't be a tick."

She raced downstairs to the kitchen where
her mum and dad were laying the table for
breakfast.

"You're up bright and early," said Dad. "Have you come to help pack the camper van?"

It was then Daisy remembered that they were going on their camping holiday today. For a moment she was so excited, she forgot why she had come downstairs.

"Shall I get the surfboard?" she asked, "and the snorkels and masks?"

"That would be good," said Dad, looking at her pyjamas. "But maybe the first thing you should get is … dressed."

"Have some breakfast first," said Mum. "I'll make some more toast."

The thought of toast reminded Daisy what she had come down for. She opened the fridge, took out a bottle of fizzy orange and headed back upstairs again.

"Fizzy pop for breakfast?" said Mum. "I'm not sure that's a good idea."

"Absolutely not," said Dad.

He opened the fridge and peered inside.

"I don't suppose there's any left, is there?"

"Hold still, Harry," said Daisy, picking up the little sparrow in her left hand.

Harry coughed and looked up at her. "Will it hurt?" he asked.

"Not at all," replied Daisy, "although it might make your beak go a bit fizzy for a while. Ready?"

Harry nodded and shut his eyes as Daisy tipped the first few drops into his beak.

At first, nothing happened. Then Harry gave a little squawk and began to dance around on Daisy's hand, flapping his wings and chirruping loudly.

"Is he all right?" asked Flapperton. "He seems a bit ... bonkers."

"That's just the fizz,"
said Daisy. "He'll be fine
in a minute."

"Whoo-hoo!" exclaimed
Harry, staggering sideways
as Daisy set him down on the
window ledge. "That one cracked
the crumbs!"

"All clear?" asked Flapperton.

"You betcha," said Harry. "Throat
clear, eyes clear, head clear. And my
beak's all bibbly-bubbly. Thanks Daisy!"

"No problem," said Daisy. "Now promise
me you'll go easy on those crumbs."

"Promise," said Harry and flew off to do
a figure of eight around the chimney pots.

"You could come and watch
us fly round the park if you like,"
said Flapperton. "I'm going
to show Harry how to
do loop the loops."

"Normally I'd love to," said Daisy, "but I'm going to the seaside today."

"The seaside?" Flapperton was quiet for a moment. Then he said, "I met some swifts once who told me stories about the sea. They used to fly thousands of miles to distant lands. And one day, when they were skimming across the sea, they flew through a rainbow and the whole sky was alive with colours. Can you imagine anything more wonderful?"

"It does sound lovely," agreed Daisy.

"The thing is," said Flapperton, "although I practise every day, I know I'll never be able to fly as far or as high as they do. But I still dream about it, Daisy. I still dream about flying through rainbows."

As he looked at her, Daisy saw the bright sky reflected in his eyes.

"Will you tell me about it?" he asked. "When you come back, will you tell me about all the things you've seen?"

Daisy smiled. "Of course I will," she said.

She watched him fly away across the
rooftops, then closed the window and
clapped her hands together.

"Right," she said. "Time to start packing!"

# Rabsy and Raberta

When they had found their spot on the campsite, Dad parked the camper van and laid the picnic table while Mum unpacked everything they'd need.

"Soon be finished, love," she said. "Then we can go down to the beach for a swim."

"Is there anything I can do to help?" asked Daisy.

"You could fetch some water," said Dad. "Then I'll put the kettle on and make us a nice cup of tea."

* * *

The campsite was on a cliff top overlooking the sea. It was a hot, blue day and, as Daisy watched the sun sparkling on the water, she imagined running across the sand towards the waves. She guessed most people were already on the beach, enjoying the warm sunshine.

She had just turned the tap on to fill the water container when she heard a little voice say, "Look. It's a magical cloud lady."

"Are you sure?" asked another voice.

"Yes. She fills the cloud with rain, puts it up in the sky and then it comes down *blib-a-loober-lub*. Like that."

Daisy turned off the tap and looked around.

"Why has she stopped?" asked
the second voice.

"Because she doesn't want it to rain
very much. She just wants it to rain on the
heads of the naughty foxes who will say
'I'm not going out rabbit-hunting in this
weather', and stay inside and not come and
eat us all up."

"She's a nice magic lady, isn't she?"

As Daisy peered beneath the trees, two
baby rabbits danced out of the shadows and
stood blinking in the sunlight.

"Hello," said Daisy, getting down on her
hands and knees so as not to frighten them.
"What are your names?"

"I'm Rabsy," said the slightly
taller of the two, "and
this is my sister
Raberta."

"Hello Magical Cloud Lady," said Raberta shyly. "Thank you for making it rain on the naughty foxes."

Daisy smiled. "I don't make it rain on the foxes," she said. She held up the water container to show them. "This is to put water in so people can drink it later."

"Like a cloud," said Raberta.

"Well … yes, I suppose so," agreed Daisy. "But clouds live up in the sky and this one's going back to my camper van."

"Won't it mind not being up with all the others?" asked Rabsy.

"I shouldn't think so," said Daisy. Then, to avoid any more questions about clouds, she took her camera from her pocket and took a picture of the sky. She turned the camera round and showed the picture to the rabbits.

"She caught them!" squeaked Raberta, hopping about with excitement. "She caught the clouds in her magical cloud-catcher!"

"Shake them out so
we can have a proper
look," said Rabsy.

"They're not really in there," Daisy
explained. "They're just pictures so you can
see them again when you get home."

"Like Rabsy, you mean?" asked Raberta.
"I always see him again when I get home.
Usually holding a carrot."

Rabsy nodded. "I like carrots," he said.

At that moment, Daisy heard her mother
calling.

"I think I'd better be getting back," she
said. "We're going surfing in a minute."

"Surfing?" asked Raberta. "What's surfing?"

"Oh it's great fun," said Daisy. "You lie on a surfboard and the waves take you all the way to the beach."

"What's a beach?" asked Raberta.

"That brown crumbly thing at the bottom of the cliff," said Rabsy.

"Oh," said Raberta. "And what are waves?"

"The blue uppy downy things."

"And what's a surfboard?"

"A foam floaty thing," said Daisy.

"Oh, right." Raberta thought for a moment. "So you lie on the foam floaty thing and look at the white cloudy things until a blue uppy downy thing takes you to the brown crumbly thing?"

"Sounds about right," said Daisy.

"Brilliant!" said Raberta. "Can me and Rabsy have a go?"

"I don't know," said Daisy. "It's not the kind of thing rabbits usually do."

"That's why we should do it," said Raberta. "I want to be the first rabbit to ride on a foam floaty thing!"

"Me too!" said Rabsy. "I want to be first too! Oh can we? Please Daisy, puh-*lease?*"

Daisy was about to say she really didn't think it would be a good idea, when she remembered how sad Flapperton the sparrow had been about the things he couldn't do. She didn't have the heart to make the rabbits sad too.

"I tell you what," she said. "If you come down to the beach tomorrow, I'll see what I can do."

"Oh fank you," said Raberta, hugging Daisy's ankle and planting rabbity kisses all over it. "Mwah, mwah, mwah!"

31

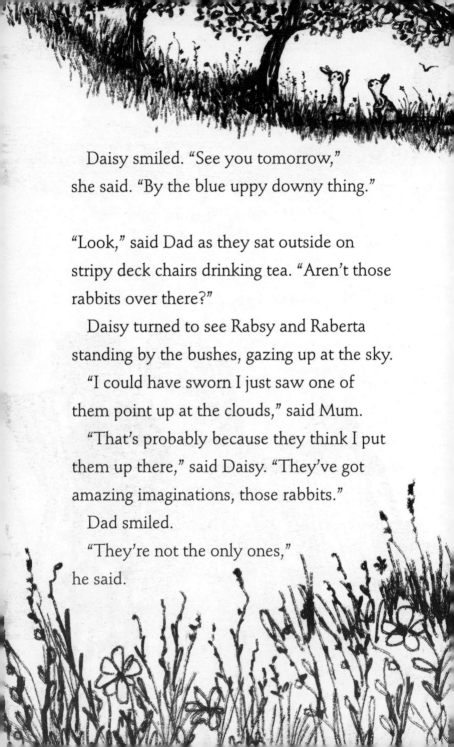

Daisy smiled. "See you tomorrow,"
she said. "By the blue uppy downy thing."

"Look," said Dad as they sat outside on
stripy deck chairs drinking tea. "Aren't those
rabbits over there?"

Daisy turned to see Rabsy and Raberta
standing by the bushes, gazing up at the sky.

"I could have sworn I just saw one of
them point up at the clouds," said Mum.

"That's probably because they think I put
them up there," said Daisy. "They've got
amazing imaginations, those rabbits."

Dad smiled.

"They're not the only ones,"
he said.

# Dancing with Pinchy

"Did you know," said Dad, staring out to sea, "that more than half of our bodies are made up of water?"

"Mine isn't," said Daisy, taking another bite of her sandwich. "At the moment mine's mostly made up of peanut butter." She stood up and looked around to see if there was any sign of the rabbits. She hadn't seen them for a couple of days and wondered if they had changed their minds about learning to surf. "Can I go swimming now?"

"You'd better finish your sandwiches first," said Mum. "Why don't you go and look in the rock pools? You never know what you might find."

As Daisy wandered across the sand, two seagulls landed nearby and stared at her.

"I-think-she's-got-some-food!" squawked the first one. "I-think-she's-got-some-food-I-bet-she's-got-some-food-I saw-her-with-some-food-where-did-she-put-her-food?"

"I-think-I-see-her-food!" squawked the second one. "I-think-I-see-her-food-I-do-I-see-her-food-I-want-to-have-her-food-and-you-can't-have-her-food!"

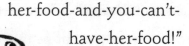

"You can both have some," said Daisy, tearing the crusts off her sandwich, "but first you have to calm down a bit or you might choke and I haven't got any fizzy drink left."

"EEK!" said the first seagull.

"ULP!" said the second one, shutting his beak with a loud clack.

"That's better," said Daisy, throwing them half a crust each.

"You're a funny looking seagull," said the first one when he had finished off his bread. "Did your feathers fall off or something?"

"I'm not a seagull," said Daisy. "I just know how to talk to animals, that's all."

"You talk funny," said the first one. "You should use the back of your throat a bit more. ARK! ARK! Like that."

"Ark! Ark!" said Daisy.

"Not bad. But you need to work on it."
The seagull waddled closer. "I don't suppose
you can talk to fish, can you?"

"I don't know," replied Daisy. "I've never
tried."

"Well you *should* try."

"She should try, shouldn't she?" said the
other seagull.

"When you get down to the sea, ask them
all to swim up to the surface."

*"Swim up to the surface,"* echoed the other
seagull.

"So you can eat them, you mean?" said
Daisy.

"ARK! ARK!" shouted the seagulls
together. "Eat-the-fish! Eat-the-fish!"

"I don't think I will, thank you," said
Daisy. "But it was nice to meet you!"

"I said that to a fish once," said the first seagull. "Nice to eat you! ARK! ARK!"

"ARK! ARK!" laughed the other seagull. "Nice-to-eat-you! Nice-to-eat-you!"

They both flew up into the air squawking, "Eat-the-fish! Eat-the-fish! Eat-the-fish! Eat-the-fish!"

"Well, really!" said Daisy, folding her arms. She thought about Flapperton and was glad that at least *some* birds had been brought up to have good manners.

Daisy sat on a rock next to a long, deep pool and dangled her feet in the water. She loved the way the tide went out and

left its treasures hidden amongst the rocks;
glassy shrimps tiptoeing across silver sand,
bright fishes darting beneath the weeds and
the tiny tentacles of sea anemones waving
like mermaids' hair in the watery breeze.

"Ow!" she said suddenly. "Owchy, ow,
ow, ow!"

Pulling her foot from the water, she saw a
small crab hanging from her toe by one of its
pincers. Carefully, she lowered her foot onto
the rock and the crab scuttled sideways.

"HA-HA!" it said, waving
its claws at her. "PINCHY,
PINCHY, PINCHY!"

"That's not very nice,"
said Daisy, rubbing her toe.

"A-what?" said the crab.

"I said it's not very nice,

going round pinching people when they're not expecting it."

"Pinchy, pinchy, pinchy," said the crab again, sidling up to Daisy's toe. "Pinchy, pinchy, pinchy!"

"Now *stop* it," said Daisy firmly, pulling her toe away. "How would you like it if I started pinching you?"

The crab stared at her. "You haven't got-a the pincers," he said.

"So?" replied Daisy. She began tapping her fingers and thumbs together, then moved them towards the crab. "Pinchy, pinchy, pinchy. Pinchy, pinchy, pinchy!"

"CARAMBA!" cried the crab, putting his claws over his head. "Stoppity, stoppity, stop-stop!"

"You see?" said Daisy, putting her hands down. "It's not very nice, is it?"

"Hokay," said the crab. "I see what-a you mean."

He looked at the rock pool for a moment as if he was about to jump back in. Then he seemed to change his mind.

"Wanna learn to walk a-sideways like-a me?" he said. "Ees fun. Ees a-sideways fun!"

"I already know how to walk sideways," said Daisy.

"No you do not," said the crab. "Not a-like a crab."

"I do too," said Daisy. She walked sideways along the edge of the rock, did a little twirl and then walked back again.

"AH-LA-LA BAMBA!" said the crab. "That was-a pretty good." He scuttled closer and stared at her. "Are you *actually* a crab?"

"No."

"But all that a-pinching and a-walking a-sideways. And, also, you speako the lingo."

"Well that's another story," said Daisy. "Talking to animals is just something I do."

"And this is a-what *I* do," said the crab,

holding out his claws. "Pinchy, pinchy, pinchy. Pinchy, pinchy, pinchy!"

He stopped and clonked his claw softly against the top of his shell as though he was thinking.

"Am a-having an idea," he said as Daisy moved her foot away. "How about I stop-a the pinching and teach-a you how to dance instead?"

Daisy smiled. "Pinchy," she said, "I think that's a *wonderful* idea."

"OK then," said Pinchy. "Watch carefully. First you put-a your claw in the air like you just don't a-care."

"You mean like this?" asked Daisy, waving a hand above her head.

"Exactly like-a-that," said Pinchy. "And now you's a-gotta feel the rhythm, Daisy. You's a-gotta listen to the wind and the waves and the earth and the sky and then you move your feet like-a-this,

and your claws like-a-this,
and then you start-a to dance!"

He clacked his claws together in a little
*ha-cha-cha* rhythm. "Come on, Daisy! Get
a-with the rhythm!"

Daisy raised her arms above her head and
began snapping her fingers, shuffling her feet
and twirling around like a flamenco dancer.

*Ha, cha, ha-cha-cha! Ha, cha, ha-cha-cha!*

"Look, Pinchy!" she cried. "I'm doing it,
I'm doing it!"

"And I'm a-loving it," said Pinchy, lifting his legs up and down in time to the rhythm. "Daisy Dawson, you's a-mekkin' me crazy!"

"Come on, Pinchy," called Daisy, still dancing. "Let's do the dance together!"

Pinchy began clacking his claws together, copying Daisy's movements and singing "Ha, cha, ha-cha-cha! Ha, cha, ha-cha-cha!"

"That's it, Pinchy!" giggled Daisy. "You've *got* it. You've got it!"

As they danced across the rock, more crabs crawled out of the water and began joining in.

*Ha, cha, ha-cha-cha! Ha, cha, ha-cha-cha!*

One started a clackety rhythm in the background, one scraped his claws rhythmically across the barnacles and another began thumping the seaweed.

The sound was so catchy that after a while even the limpets started joining in, lifting their shells up and down in time to the beat.

*Slurpy-slurp, slurpy-slurp.*

*Slurpy-slurpy-slurpy-slurp.*

*Ha, cha, ha-cha-cha! Ha, cha, ha-cha-cha!*

"Hey Daisy!" called a voice behind her. "Wotcha doin'?"

Still dancing and ha-cha-cha-ing, Daisy turned to see Rabsy and Raberta skipping about on the sand.

"Come and join us!" she called, holding out her foot so that one of the crabs could play a little solo on her toenails. Rabsy and Raberta hopped up onto the rock and, as the crabs moved back to give them some space, Raberta began to sing a little rap.

*"We're so happy by the sea,*
*Hearing all the crabs go clacker-dee-dee.*
*I'm Raberta, he's Rabsy,*
*And we're hangin' with our good friend*
*Daisy D."*

Suddenly the music stopped and all the
crabs plopped back into the water just as the
two seagulls swooped down onto the rock
shouting:

"EAT-THE-CRABS! EAT-THE-CRABS!
EAT-THE-CRABS! EAT-THE-CRABS!"

They stopped and stared at Daisy.

*"ARK! ARK! We lost our food!*
*Ark! Ark! Well that's no good!*
*Ark! Lunch! We came too late!*
*Ark! Ark! Well that's just great."*

Then they flew away again.

"Sorry about that," said Daisy. "I don't think anyone's ever taught them to be polite."

"I don't think anyone's ever taught them how to rap either," said Raberta. "That was rubbish."

"I quite liked the *Ark! Ark!* bit," said Rabsy, skipping from foot to foot. Then he saw the way Raberta was looking at him and added, "But yours was *much* better."

Daisy looked around to see if anyone had noticed the dancing crabs, but everyone seemed too busy swimming or sunbathing to pay any attention.

"Splosh!" said Rabsy as a wave swept into the rock pool. "The blue uppy downy thing's come to say hello!"

"The tide's coming in," said Daisy. "Stay here a sec and I'll see if I'm allowed to go surfing."

\* \* \*

"How are the peanut butter sandwiches?" asked Dad, who was lying down reading a newspaper.

"I think they've disappeared," said Daisy, picking up her surfboard.

"Good heavens," said Dad. "I think there must be magic in the air."

Daisy smiled. "I think there is," she said.

"Well just you be careful," said Mum. "Do you want one of us to come with you?"

"No, I'll be fine," said Daisy, who knew that trying to explain about surfing rabbits would make life rather complicated. "I've got my lifesaver badge, remember?"

It was true. Daisy was one of the best swimmers in her class and had come first in the swimming gala for three years running.

But even so, her parents always wanted to make sure that she was safe.

"All right," said her mum. "But stay where we can see you and don't go out of your depth!"

When Daisy reached the sea, the tide had already flooded the rock pools and Rabsy and Raberta were standing by the waterline playing keepy-uppy with a pebble.

"You brought the foam floaty thing!" said Raberta.

"I did," said Daisy. "So who wants a ride on the blue uppy downy thing?"

"Me!" shouted both rabbits together, jumping up and down on the sand.

"OK," said Daisy, "but first you need to calm down a bit."

"Sorry," said Raberta. She stopped jumping up and down and then held onto Rabsy's ears until he stopped too.

"Now," said Daisy, "first of all we need to

go through some safety procedures."

"Do not talk to foxes," said Raberta sternly. "NEVER talk to foxes."

"OK, good," said Daisy, "although I was thinking more about surfing actually."

She did a quick check to make sure no one was watching, then waved the two rabbits towards the front of the surfboard.

"Now go like this," she said, holding her arms out.

As Rabsy and Raberta raised their front paws, Rabsy started swaying from side to side, pretending to lose his balance.

"Uh oh," he said. "Going … left! Going … right!"

"Rabsy, pay attention," said Daisy. "When we're riding the waves, that's when you can have a go at standing up. But you have to put your paws out to help you balance. And remember, any time you think you're about to fall off, just lie down and hang on to me."

"Where will you be?" asked Raberta nervously.

"Right behind you," said Daisy. "Now let's have a little practice. When I say 'Surf' you stand up and put your paws out, and when I say 'Drop' you lie down and pretend to be holding my arms. Are you ready?"

"Ready," said Rabsy.

"Ready," said Raberta.

"OK, and... Surf!"

Rabsy and Raberta jumped to the front of the board and held their paws out just as they had been shown.

"And ... drop!"

Rabsy and Raberta
dropped to the board with a little
"Ooof!" sound.

"Now pretend to be holding my arms,"
Daisy reminded them. "That's it, that's it,
and ... surf! And ... drop! And ... surf! And
... drop!"

Rabsy rolled off the board and lay on his
back in the sand. "I'm tired now," he said.
"Can't we play hide and squeak instead?"

Daisy chewed her lip and looked out to sea. Although she was a strong swimmer, she could see that the waves were a bit rough and she didn't want to put the little rabbits in any danger.

"Perhaps we'd better leave it until tomorrow," she said.

"Phew," said Rabsy, lying on his back and staring up at the sky.

"Surf's up tomorrow though, li'l brother," said Raberta, grabbing his ears and pulling him to his feet. "What d'you think, Daisy? D'you think we'll be ready to ride on the wobblers?"

Daisy smiled.

"There's only one way to find out," she said.

# Dolphin in Danger

The next morning, Daisy met Rabsy and Raberta by the rock pools.

"I'm feeding the fish," said Rabsy, dropping bits of carrot into the water.

"I don't think fish like carrots," said Daisy.

"This one does," said Rabsy. "It's waving at me."

Daisy smiled. "That's not a fish," she explained, "it's a sea anemone. It's waving its arms about because it's trying to catch some food."

"Lucky I was here then really," said Rabsy. "Can we go surfing now?"

Daisy looked at the sea and saw that the water was much calmer than the day before. "All right," she said. "But remember the safety procedures."

"We will!" chorused the rabbits. "Surf and drop! Surf and drop!"

As Daisy pushed the surfboard through the shallows, Rabsy and Raberta sat at the front and watched the waves gently rising and falling.

"Here comes another!" called Rabsy, clapping his paws together as Raberta squealed with excitement. "And another! And another!"

Raberta began skipping around the surfboard, singing a little song.

*"We can dance and we can hop*
*We can surf and we can drop*
*But if you want to surf like me*
*You must be safe beside the sea*

*So don't go where it's rough or deep*
*These are rules you have to keep."*

"Very good Raberta," said Daisy, "but you're a bit near the edge."

"Oops, sorry," said Raberta, skipping back towards the middle of the board. "Got a bit carried away there."

When Daisy was up to her waist in water, she turned to face the beach. Rabsy and Raberta stood at the end of the surfboard, lifting their paws just the way Daisy had shown them.

"Is this right?" squeaked Raberta. "Are we doing it right, Daisy?"

"That's perfect," said Daisy. "OK, ready? Here we go!"

As the ocean swelled behind her, Daisy lay on the surfboard until her arms were either side of the two little rabbits and then launched herself forward. For a moment they hung on the crest of the wave, perfectly balanced between sea and sky. Then the wave broke and they shot forward, bouncing and skimming across the water as it frothed and foamed beneath them.

"Wooooh!" cried Rabsy. "Wheeeee!"

"Drop Rabsy, drop!" shouted Raberta, throwing herself forward and clinging onto Daisy's arm. But Rabsy was having so much fun that he forgot to hang on, and when the board crashed down again he was flung off into the waves.

"Rabsy fell off!" wailed Raberta as the wave took them up the beach. "We have to go back and rescue him!"

"You stay here," said Daisy firmly. Racing back into the water, she searched frantically for the little rabbit, but all she could see was the white waves and the sunlight sparkling on the sea.

Daisy held her breath and put her face in the water, then opened her eyes, desperately searching for him. But the waves had stirred up the sand and the salt water stung her eyes, making it impossible to see.

She was about to lift her head out of the water when she thought she heard a faint voice calling, *Help me! Help me, please!*

But when she listened again, all she could hear was the sound of the sea.

"Rabsy!" she called as she raised her head. "Rabsy, where are you?"

"Right here," said a little voice behind her. "Can I have a lift, please?"

Daisy turned to see a bedraggled Rabsy paddling through the waves with wet fur plastered over his eyes.

"Rabsy!" she cried, scooping him up in her arms. "I thought I'd lost you!"

"I thought I'd lost me too," said Rabsy. "But it turns out I was here all the time."

"I heard you calling for help," said Daisy as she waded through the shallows towards the beach.

"Nah, that wasn't me," said Rabsy, "I knew you'd come and find me." He shivered and then clapped his paws together. "That was brilliant! Can we do it again?"

"I think you should get warm first," said Daisy, putting him down on the sand next to Raberta. Raberta squeaked, flung her arms around him and hugged him tight.

As the two rabbits scampered off towards the dunes to dry off in the sun, Daisy walked back up the beach to fetch her snorkel and mask.

"You looked as if you were enjoying your surfing," said Mum. "Although I could have sworn I saw something on the front of your surfboard."

"That was the rabbits," said Daisy. "They wanted to go surfing, but one of them fell off and I had to rescue him."

Mum smiled. "You and your imagination," she said.

When Daisy reached the sea, she lay on her tummy and peered down into the water. It was clearer now, and with the mask on she could see shoals of silver fish darting above the sea bed. As she listened, she heard the voice again, echoing up from the depths of the ocean. "Help me," it called. "Help me, please!"

As Daisy watched patterns of sunlight dancing on the sand beneath her, she noticed that the sea bed shelved down into deeper, darker water. And there, lying in the shadows, was a young dolphin. It had somehow got caught in an old fishing net and the more it struggled, the more it became entangled.

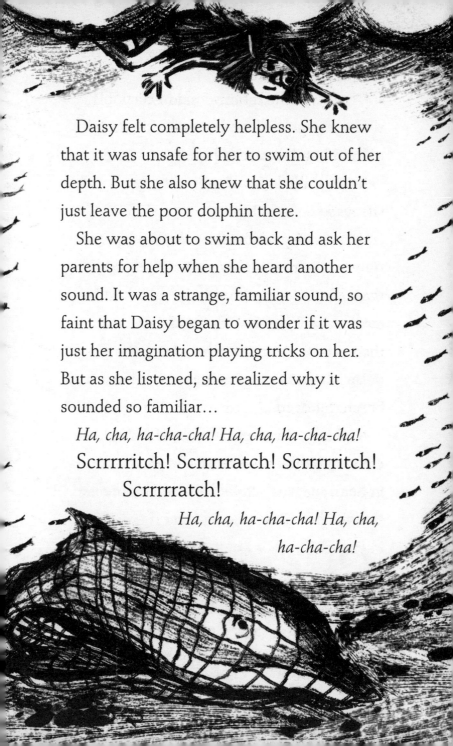

Daisy felt completely helpless. She knew that it was unsafe for her to swim out of her depth. But she also knew that she couldn't just leave the poor dolphin there.

She was about to swim back and ask her parents for help when she heard another sound. It was a strange, familiar sound, so faint that Daisy began to wonder if it was just her imagination playing tricks on her. But as she listened, she realized why it sounded so familiar…

*Ha, cha, ha-cha-cha! Ha, cha, ha-cha-cha!* Scrrrrritch! Scrrrrratch! Scrrrrritch! Scrrrrratch!

*Ha, cha, ha-cha-cha! Ha, cha, ha-cha-cha!*

Turning around, Daisy swam as fast as she could towards the sound of clacking claws. In the shallow water she saw a huge assortment of crabs gathered in a circle beneath the waves. There were crabs of all shapes and sizes, from the tiniest hermit crab to a red spider crab with a huge front claw and a barnacle-encrusted shell. All of them were dancing and singing and clacking their claws in time with the music. And there, conducting the others from the middle of the circle, was someone who looked very familiar indeed.

"Pinchy!" she cried. "Pinchy it's me, Daisy!" Although because she had a snorkel in her mouth, it actually sounded more like, "Himp-shee! Mit's me, Nayzee!"

But it didn't matter, because as all the other crabs stopped dancing and turned to see what the fuss was about, Pinchy held up his claw and waved to her.

Deciding it would be impossible to explain the situation with her snorkel in her mouth, Daisy swam down to the sea bed and held out her hand. Seeming to understand, Pinchy scuttled sideways until he was sitting on her palm, and Daisy swam to the surface again and took the snorkel out of her mouth.

"Pinchy, you've got to help me," she said.

"But a-why?" asked Pinchy. "You's a good dancer already."

"I'm not talking about dancing," said Daisy. "I'm talking about rescuing a dolphin."

"This is a joke?" asked Pinchy. "I don't a-get it."

"No, I'm being serious," said Daisy. "There's a dolphin caught in a net at the bottom of the sea and he needs our help."

"CARAMBA!" said Pinchy. "But Pinchy has a-never rescued the dolphin before."

"I'd never danced the cha-cha before either," said Daisy. "But thanks to you I'm pretty good at it now."

"Is a-true." Pinchy clacked his claws and did a little two-step shuffle on her hand. "Hokay. Let me a-go and talk to the others."

"Please don't be long," said Daisy. "I don't think we've got much time."

Pinchy scuttled off her hand and plopped back into the water. As Daisy watched him sink to the bottom again she felt a chill run through her and, looking up, she saw that the sun had gone behind a cloud. The sea had turned from blue to grey and the world suddenly seemed much darker. When Daisy looked back into the water again, all she could see was swirling sand.

Daisy decided she had better swim back and tell her parents about the dolphin. They would know what to do, wouldn't they? They always knew what to do. But as she turned towards the beach, something in the distance caught her eye.

Just around the corner on a small rocky beach, two grey dots were huddled together beneath the cliffs. They were surrounded by water and as Daisy watched, she realized to her horror that the two dots were actually Rabsy and Raberta. Somehow they had managed to get cut off in a small cove and the tide was still coming in.

In a few minutes, the beach where they stood would be completely underwater.

# Rescuing Rabbits

Without stopping to think, Daisy put her
mask back on and swam as hard as she
could towards the cliffs.

"Daisy! Daisy!" shouted the little rabbits
when they saw her. "We're over here!"

"So I see," said Daisy, stumbling out of
the water. "But what on earth are you doing
here?"

"It was Rabsy's idea," said Raberta. "I said
we should wait until you came back, but
Rabsy said it would be all right because he

was the best rabbity wave rider in the whole wide world."

"I am too," said Rabsy.

"Uh, I don't think so," said Raberta. "The best rabbity wave riders don't crash into rocks, Rabsy."

"I don't understand," said Daisy. "You haven't even got a surfboard."

"I did have," said Rabsy, pointing to a piece of wood that was lying next to the rocks, "but it sort of snapped."

"You went surfing on *that?*"

"I wouldn't call it surfing," said Raberta. "More like sinking, really."

Daisy looked at the rising water and remembered that the two little rabbits couldn't swim. It was up to her to save them.

"Climb onto my shoulders," she instructed. "I'm going to wade past the rocks and then swim round to the beach. But whatever you do, don't let go, OK?"

"OK," said Rabsy and Raberta. Daisy knelt down and they scampered up onto her shoulders.

"All set?" Daisy asked, as their little paws clutched at her hair.

"All set," said Rabsy and Raberta.

"OK," said Daisy. "Then let's go!"

As the water came up to her waist Daisy took a deep breath, pulled down her mask and launched herself forward into the sea. The rabbits clung to her neck and Daisy could feel them shivering.

"Are we nearly there?" whispered Rabsy. "I need to go and check on my carrots."

"Soon be there," said Daisy, trying to reassure him.

But although she was a strong swimmer, she began to worry that the little rabbits wouldn't have the strength to hold on much longer. The sun was behind the clouds and the beach was still some way off. As she looked around, all she could see was dark water on all sides and grey sky above her.

Then, in the distance, a shaft of sunlight broke through the clouds.

Daisy thought of home then, of her best friend Boom and the sun-bright meadow behind her house. And as the water sparkled and shone like a thousand diamonds, Daisy remembered what Boom had said to her before she left.

*If you swim towards the sun, you'll find your way home.*

For some reason she couldn't explain, Daisy began to feel braver and stronger. Then, as she swam closer to the sunlit water, Rabsy shouted, "Look! Down there!" and Daisy noticed that something was moving beneath them. It gradually rose up from the depths of the ocean, faster and faster, and then suddenly Daisy felt herself being lifted out of the water. As she looked down,

she realized to her
surprise that she was riding on
the back of a dolphin.

"Oh!" she cried happily. "Where did *you* come from?"

The dolphin flicked its tail, crested a wave and swam smoothly into calmer waters.

"I wanted to see you," said the dolphin, and when it spoke Daisy thought it was like listening to the most beautiful music she had ever heard. "I wanted to thank you for telling the crabs I was in trouble. They came in their hundreds to free me from the net, and so now you must tell me what I can do for you in return."

"Perhaps you could take us back to the beach," said Daisy. "If it's not too much trouble."

"For you, nothing is too much trouble," replied the dolphin. "But perhaps you would like to come for a little ride first?"

"Yes please," whispered Daisy.

As the dolphin leapt through the waves, Daisy held on tight and watched the water rushing past. But although they were moving at great speed, the dolphin swam so smoothly that Daisy felt as if she was sliding through fields of blue silk. High above her, the clouds gave way to clear skies and Daisy felt the warm sun on her back once again. Then, as they splashed across the tops of the waves,

Rabsy and Raberta squealed
with delight, and Daisy turned to see
tiny rainbows dancing in the spray all
around them.

"They've got green grass in them!"
shouted Rabsy, pointing at the bright colours
shimmering above the sea. "And yellow sun
and blue sky and everything!"

Far below them, tiny fish swam through
secret caves and played hide and seek in
forests of blue and green seaweed. As the
dolphin turned back towards the shore,
a group of swifts flew alongside them,
skimming the bright water before soaring
up into the summer sky. Daisy thought of
Flapperton sitting on the window ledge and
dreaming of rainbows.

"That was wonderful," she said as the dolphin stopped in the shallows. She stroked the dolphin's smooth back and stared out towards the horizon. "The sea is very big," she whispered. "Will you be all right out there on your own?"

"I won't be on my own," said the dolphin. "Listen."

Daisy leaned sideways until her ear was touching the water and, from somewhere far away, she heard the faintest of clicking sounds.

She smiled. "Are those your friends?"

The dolphin nodded. "They're singing because you found me," he said. "And now they are calling me home."

As Daisy and the rabbits waved goodbye to the dolphin, Daisy noticed something fall off its tail into the water. Bending down, she scooped it up and there, sitting in the palm of her hand, was Pinchy the crab.

"Pinchy!" she cried. "What are you doing?"

Pinchy looked up at her and clacked his claws together. "My grandfather crab, he tell me that a-riding on a dolphin is-a full of the magic. So I hitch-a myself a ride."

"And what did you think?"

Pinchy raised a claw and clacked it like a castanet. "Is a-magic all right," he said. "Pinchy very happy."

He held out his other claw and Daisy saw that he was holding a small piece of glass that had been washed smooth by the sea.

"Is a gift," he said, "for a-you."

Then with a cry of "Keep a-dancing, Daisy!" he scuttled to the edge of her hand, jumped into the water and disappeared beneath the waves.

"I wonder what it's for?" said Daisy, turning the glass over in her hand.

"Maybe it's so you don't forget us when you go home again," said Raberta.

Daisy stroked her silky ears. "I'll never do that," she said. Then, noticing that both rabbits were still shivering, she gathered them up in her arms and took them to a sunny spot next to the cliff path.

"The walk home should warm you up," she told them. "But if you're still cold, just remember what Pinchy said: 'Keep a-dancing!'"

Rabsy and Raberta giggled and hugged Daisy's legs. Then they set off up the cliff path, dancing and waving until finally they were lost from sight.

"I always knew you were a good swimmer," said Dad, wrapping Daisy in a towel, "but I didn't know you were *that* good."

"What do you mean?" asked Daisy.

"You looked as though you were riding on a speedboat." Dad chuckled. "I think you must have been caught by a wave or something. But the funny thing was, you looked as though you had a couple of fluffy toys on there with you."

Mum packed away the picnic basket and shook her head. "I think your Dad's been sitting in the sun too long," she said.

"I think he has," said Daisy. "I mean, it's obvious that Rabsy and Raberta are rabbits."

"Eh?" said Dad.

Daisy rolled up her towel and smiled. "Never mind," she said.

As they walked back up the beach, she felt the smooth glass in her pocket.

"Can we stop at the shop on the way home?" she asked. "I just need to get some presents for my friends."

"That's very thoughtful of you," said Mum. "What did you have in mind?"

"Carrot juice," said Daisy, "and maybe some hazelnut ice cream."

"Those are some interesting choices," said Dad.

Daisy smiled.

"I've got some interesting friends," she said.

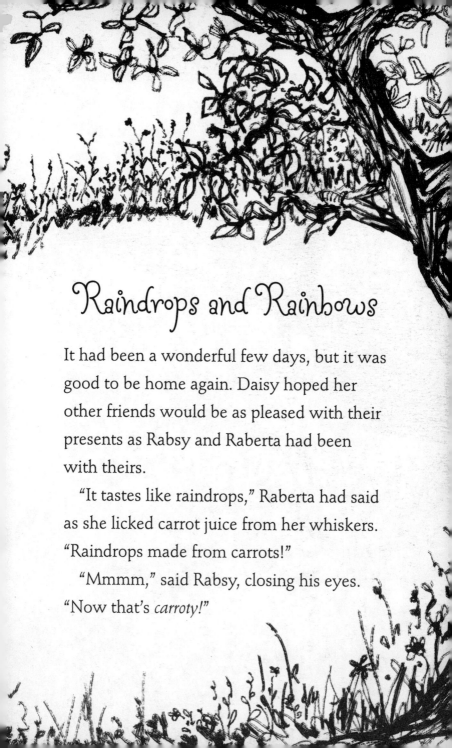

# Raindrops and Rainbows

It had been a wonderful few days, but it was good to be home again. Daisy hoped her other friends would be as pleased with their presents as Rabsy and Raberta had been with theirs.

"It tastes like raindrops," Raberta had said as she licked carrot juice from her whiskers. "Raindrops made from carrots!"

"Mmmm," said Rabsy, closing his eyes. "Now that's *carroty!*"

As Daisy walked down the lane listening to the bees buzz amongst the flowers, she heard Boom discussing the weather with Meadowsweet the mare.

"The thing about sunshine," he was saying, "is that it's mainly warm and dry. Whereas rain, on the whole, is a good deal wetter."

"Can't argue with that," said Meadowsweet, looking up at the blue sky. "Although I rather like the taste of grass after rain. It makes my breath feel fresh and cool."

As Daisy leaned on the gate, Meadowsweet turned and stamped her foot with delight. "Look who's home again!" she whinnied.

"Hello Meadowsweet," replied Daisy happily. "How would you like something to make your breath feel fresh and cool right now?"

"I wouldn't say no," replied Meadowsweet, trotting over to the gate. "What have you got? Rain in a bag?"

"Not exactly," said Daisy. "But I think you might like it anyway."

She pulled a peppermint from her pocket and offered it to Meadowsweet. Boom watched with interest as Meadowsweet gently snuffled it out of Daisy's hand.

"How does it taste?" he asked.

"Hang on," said Meadowsweet. She chomped on the mint and shivered. "It's like a cold drink from a snowy stream, but without the wet parts. It's delicious, Daisy!"

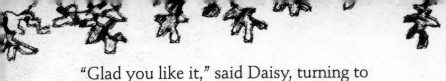

"Glad you like it," said Daisy, turning to Boom. "I've got something for you too."

She pulled out a small grey pebble and offered it to him through the gate.

Boom stared at it, sniffed it and then looked back at Daisy. "Not being funny or anything, but what do I do with it?"

"You eat it," said Daisy.

"Oh," said Boom, sounding disappointed. "The thing is, I don't really like eating pebbles. I tried one once and my teeth nearly fell out."

Daisy laughed. "It's not a real one, silly," she said. "It's a peanut butter pebble. I bought a bag of them from the gift shop near the beach."

Boom sniffed at the pebble again and licked his lips. "It *does* smell good," he said.

He stared at the pebble
for a while longer. Then he
took it from Daisy's hand, crunched
it up and swallowed it. "Oh my,"
he said. "Oh my, oh my, oh *my*."

Daisy giggled. "You like
it then?"

Boom shook his
head. "The word *like*,"
he said, "does not do justice to what
is happening in my mouth right now."

At that moment Hazel and Conker
came scampering down from the oak tree,
squeaking, "Daisy's home, Daisy's home!"

"Hello small squirrels," said Daisy.
"I've brought a present for you too." She
reached into her bag and pulled out the
little tub of hazelnut ice cream she had
bought on the way home. It was already
starting to go soft in the heat, but it was
still quite cold.

"It's a hat!" exclaimed Hazel as Daisy peeled back the lid. "A hat full of squishy stuff."

"It's not a hat," said Daisy. "It's ice cream."

Conker dipped his nose in and squealed. "It's like those things that fall down in winter!" he cried.

"What, ducks you mean?" asked Hazel. "Ducks falling over on the ice?"

"No, not ducks. The stuff that comes out of the sky."

"Ducks come out of the sky," said Hazel. "They come out of the sky like anything."

"Snow," said Conker, licking the end of his nose. "It's like snow, but with nuts in it!"

"Nutty snow!" cried Hazel excitedly. She scooped out some ice cream, popped it in her mouth, then jumped in the air and ran off around the water trough.

"She always does that when she's excited," explained Conker. "First time she tried a cashew nut she went round it twenty-six times."

After a few more circuits, Hazel skipped back across the field, put her paws above her head and fell back into the long grass.

"I lubbety-*lub* ice cream," she said, staring up at the sky.

"I thought you might," said Daisy, delighted that her presents had been such a success. But then she remembered something.

"Excuse me," she said, "but I think there's someone else I need to see."

Back in her bedroom, Daisy flung open the window and watched the swifts twisting and turning in the cloudless sky.

Bees buzzed and bumbled
in the flower beds,
humming sweet
songs about honey.
As the sun warmed
her face, she closed
her eyes and felt a soft
breeze in her hair. Then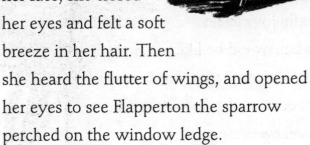
she heard the flutter of wings, and opened
her eyes to see Flapperton the sparrow
perched on the window ledge.

 "Hello Daisy," he
said, "you look happy.
Did you have lots of
adventures?"

"As a matter of fact,
I did," said Daisy. Flapperton's eyes grew
wider and wider as she told him about all
the things she had done.

"But did you fly through any rainbows?"
he asked when she had finished.

"Sort of," said Daisy, remembering the tiny rainbows she had seen on her dolphin ride.

"You are so lucky," said Flapperton. "I would love to do that. It would be like a dream come true. But," he added sadly, "I don't think it will ever happen."

"Well you never know," said Daisy. "Life is full of surprises. Like the other day, for instance, someone gave me a present and I didn't know what it was for. But then this morning when I opened the curtains, I found out."

She took the piece of glass that Pinchy had given to her and held it up to the light. And as a shimmering patch of colours appeared on the window ledge, she smiled and said,

"It's for you, Flapperton. It's your very own rainbow."

And as Flapperton began to flutter back and forth through the bright colours that hovered in the warm summer air, Daisy thought about the rabbits, and the dancing crabs, and the dolphin swimming out towards the open sea.

She realized then that there was far more magic in the world than most people ever dreamed of.

You just had to know where to look.

Steve Voake is the author of five novels for older readers including *The Dreamwalker's Child,* and also writes the Hooey Higgins series for Walker. This is his fourth Daisy Dawson book. He says, "My daughter Daisy loves animals, and when she was little, she was always having conversations with them. I imagined what it would be like if they started talking back to her – and that's how Daisy Dawson was born!"

Steve lives in Somerset.

Jessica Meserve is the author and illustrator of the picture books *Small, Can Anybody Hear Me?* and *Bedtime without Arthur.* She has illustrated several other titles including *Drawing Together* by Mimi Thebo, *Grandad and John* by Jeanne Willis and the previous Daisy Dawson books. She says, "As a girl I wished I could talk to animals too. I love illustrating Daisy because she lets me have those adventures as a grown-up."